FOR THOMAS

Once upon a time,
About 6 months ago,
There was a boy who couldn't poo,
His story you might know.

Previously a happy child,
Now Thomas wore a frown.
His smile was scarcely ever seen
Unless if upside down.

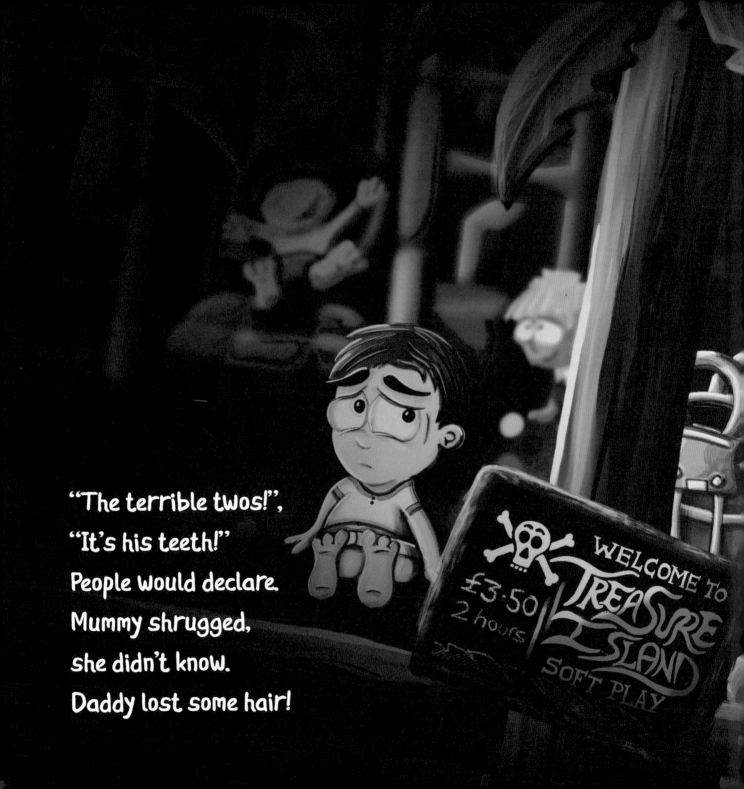

"The terrible twos!",
"It's his teeth!"
People would declare.
Mummy shrugged,
she didn't know.
Daddy lost some hair!

Mum and Dad were worried now,
The stress began to show.
Nothing that they could think to do
Could make poor Thomas go.

They went to see the Wizard,
At a house by the woods.
Who better now to help Thomas
Deliver his late goods?

He rummaged in his kitchen
Looking for a cure.
There were jars and vials
of wondrous things
Behind each cupboard door.

Finally he found something,
"Ah ha, now that's the bag!
Eat these magic sweets, my boy,
They'll make your nappy sag!"

Thomas had a little bite,
Then he scoffed them all
Sixty seconds after that
He's running down the hall.

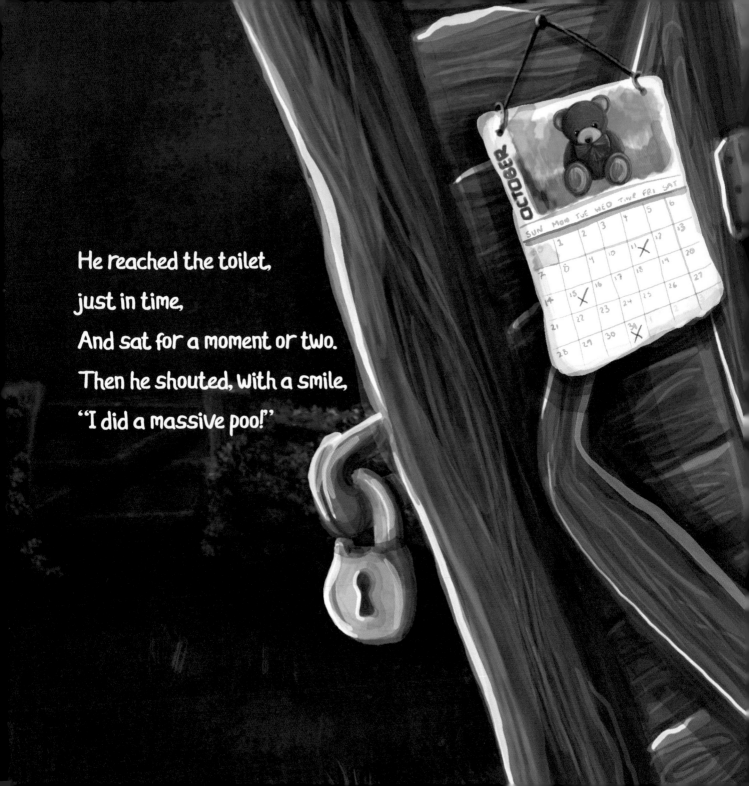

He reached the toilet,
just in time,
And sat for a moment or two.
Then he shouted, with a smile,
"I did a massive poo!"

Daddy shook the wizard's hand,
Mummy gave him money.
Thomas felt much better now,
And so did his poor tummy!

Craig Mitchell is a British children's author who was born in 1983.

Originally from Bolton, Lancashire (up North), he moved to the East Midlands with his parent when he was 4 years old. The stories Craig writes are inspired by his son Thomas, with whom he lives in rural Leicestershire.

If you enjoyed this book you may also like 'The Boy Who Couldn't Burp' which was Craig's first book which he published in 2018.

Printed in Poland
by Amazon Fulfillment
Poland Sp. z o.o., Wrocław